It's a Wonderful Life for Kids!

JIMMY HAWKINS

Illustrations by DOUGLAS B. JONES

Dutton Children's Books

DUTTON CHILDREN'S BOOKS
A division of Penguin Young Readers Group

Published by the Penguin Group
Penguin Group (USA) Inc., 375 Hudson Street, New York, New York 10014, U.S.A.
Penguin Group (Canada), 90 Eglinton Avenue East, Suite 700, Toronto, Ontario, Canada M4P 2Y3
(a division of Pearson Penguin Canada Inc.) • Penguin Books Ltd, 80 Strand, London WC2R 0RL, England
Penguin Ireland, 25 St Stephen's Green, Dublin 2, Ireland (a division of Penguin Books Ltd)
Penguin Group (Australia), 250 Camberwell Road, Camberwell, Victoria 3124, Australia (a division of Pearson
Australia Group Pty Ltd) • Penguin Books India Pvt Ltd, 11 Community Centre, Panchsheel Park, New Delhi - 110 017, India
Penguin Group (NZ), Cnr Airborne and Rosedale Roads, Albany, Auckland 1310, New Zealand (a division of Pearson
New Zealand Ltd) • Penguin Books (South Africa) (Pty) Ltd, 24 Sturdee Avenue, Rosebank, Johannesburg 2196, South Africa
Penguin Books Ltd, Registered Offices: 80 Strand, London WC2R 0RL, England

Library of Congress Cataloging-in-Publication Data

Hawkins, Jimmy.
It's a wonderful life for kids! / by Jimmy Hawkins; illustrated by Douglas B. Jones.—1st ed.   p. cm.
Summary: Based on the movie *It's a Wonderful Life*, George and Mary Bailey's eight-year-old son Tommy
gets some help from an angel-in-training named Arthur.
ISBN 0-525-47767-5 (alk. paper)
[1. Angels—Fiction.] I. Jones, Douglas B., ill. II. Title. III. Title: It is a wonderful life for kids.
PZ7.H313516Its 2006   [Fic]—dc22   2006004192

It's a Wonderful Life is a trademark owned by Republic Entertainment Inc.®,
a subsidiary of Spelling Entertainment Group Inc.®

Published in the United States by Dutton Children's Books,
a division of Penguin Young Readers Group
345 Hudson Street, New York, New York 10014
www.penguin.com/youngreaders

Designed by Sara Reynolds and Abby Kuperstock
Manufactured in China
First Edition
1 3 5 7 9 10 8 6 4 2

Author's Note

On December 20, 1946, the film *It's a Wonderful Life* premiered at the Globe Theatre in New York City. It starred two Academy Award-winning actors, James Stewart and Donna Reed. A ticket cost $1.25. The movie received many positive reviews and five Academy Award nominations. Ultimately, however, it was a disappointment for its producer and director, Frank Capra. It didn't win any Oscars, and it ended up losing $480,000 for Liberty Films, Inc.

The copyright was sold to Republic Pictures and was not renewed when the appropriate time came, in 1974. The film fell into public domain, which meant that any television station could show it without paying a fee. Beginning in the late 1970s, the movie was aired countless times across America. Thus *It's a Wonderful Life* became a classic. Many families have made viewing it one of their indispensable holiday traditions. The film offers enduring and universal messages of hope, charity, and life renewed. George Bailey learns with the help of Clarence, his guardian angel, that "no man is a failure who has friends."

I was fortunate enough to play the character of Tommy Bailey (George and Mary's youngest child) when I was four and a half years old. After we finished making the movie, I remained in touch with many members of the cast. We felt blessed to be a part of *It's a Wonderful Life*, and seeing its popularity grow over the years has been heartwarming, to say the least. In honor of the film's sixtieth anniversary, I wrote a story inspired by the original. It has the same kind of inspirational messages, but this time the focus is on Tommy Bailey. I wanted to show young readers that everyone's life, no matter how old he or she may be, makes a difference. I hope you enjoy this homage to Frank Capra's magical film.

Jimmy Hawkins

To Mikey and Scottie

—J.H.

Acknowledgments

I'm indebted to Lloyd J. Schwartz for his valued advice . . . Eileen Wesson for her encouragement. Gratitude to Dee Ann . . . Doug Whiteman for believing. Great respect to Stephanie Owens Lurie for her creative guidance. Special thanks to Doug Jones for making Bedford Falls and its characters come to life in his wonderful illustrated world.

A very worried George and Mary Bailey were praying for their son Tommy's safe return.

"Please bring Tommy home," said his sister Zuzu.

Their pleas were heard way up in Heaven.

"Looks like we'll have to send somebody down," said one angel.

"I know this family," said an angel named Clarence. "I think Arthur should handle this one."

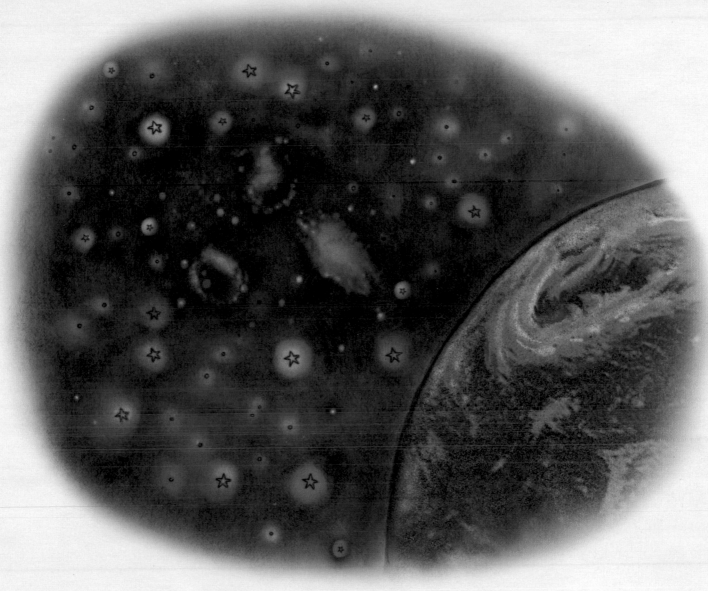

In a flash, a third angel joined them. "You sent for me, sir?"

"Yes, Arthur. An eleven-year-old boy on Earth needs your help," said Clarence. "He's thinking of running away from home. He's scared, very scared."

"Sir, if I accomplish my mission, will I get my wings? It has been 205 years . . ."

"Arthur, I asked that very same question once. You do a good job with Tommy Bailey, and you'll get your wings. If you're to help, you'll want to know something about him. Now, look down there . . ."

"But I can't see."

"Oh, I forgot, you haven't got your wings yet. There. Now can you see anything?"

"Why, yes, this is amazing!"

"That's the Bailey house at 320 Sycamore," said Clarence.

"Oh, they're having a Christmas party," said Arthur. "They all look so happy. Except that boy touching the wall—who's that?"

"That's your problem," said Clarence. "Tommy Bailey, back when he was four."

The wall felt strangely hot to Tommy. He made his way through the crowd to his dad and yanked on his coat. "'Scuse me, 'scuse me," he said.

"Excuse you for what?" asked his father.

"The wall is really hot, Daddy," said Tommy.

"Don't bother Daddy, Tommy. He's busy," said his brother, Pete.

Concerned, George followed Tommy to the wall and laid his hand on it. Then he called over Bert the cop to examine it, too.

"It looks like something's wrong," said Arthur. "What is it?"

"You'll see," said Clarence. "First, let's take a look at Tommy a little later, when he is seven years old."

As Tommy swept the floor at Gower Drugs, he talked to a regular customer sitting alone at a table.

"I see you here all the time," Tommy said to the woman. "You must really like ice cream. My name's Tommy Bailey."

The woman smiled. "Pleased to meet you, Tommy. I'm Mrs. Davis. And, yes, I like ice cream." She lowered her voice to a whisper. "But, to tell you the truth, the real reason I come here is to see Mr. Gower. He seems like such a nice man."

"He is," Tommy agreed. "He gives me free ice cream for sweeping up." Tommy looked toward the counter, where Mr. Gower was working. "I wish I could cheer him up, though. He's been real sad since his wife died."

"I know how that is," Mrs. Davis said with a sigh.

Just then Mr. Gower came over. "Well, Tommy, you've done a fine job. What flavor will it be?"

"Vanilla, please. Oh, and say hi to Mrs. Davis. She thinks you're nice."

"Tommy, I didn't ask you to introduce me to Mr. Gower. I'm so embarrassed!"

"I'm glad he said something," said Mr. Gower. "I've noticed you, too. I'll be closing as soon as I make Tommy his cone. Then would you care to go for a walk?"

"Yes, I'd like that," said Mrs. Davis.

"Because of Tommy's introduction," Clarence told Arthur, *"Mr. Gower and Mrs. Davis eventually got married. Now watch this, Arthur. Tommy is nine, and he has a paper route."*

One very hot summer day, Mrs. Carter offered Tommy a glass of lemonade. As they were talking, Mrs. Carter started gasping for air. Then she asked for help.

Without hesitation Tommy ran into the street to flag down a passing car. "You gotta help, mister!" Tommy yelled to the driver.

The man pulled over and rushed to Mrs. Carter, while Tommy went inside to call the doctor.

In a few minutes, Mrs. Carter was feeling better again. Tommy and the man waited until the doctor arrived before going their separate ways. A very grateful Mrs. Carter waved good-bye.

"I don't understand," said Arthur. "Tommy is obviously a very good boy. Why would he want to run away?"

"We're getting there," said Clarence. "Now Tommy is eleven. He's been collecting money from the sixth graders for a library fund."

"Wow," said Tommy, counting the money in the envelope. "We've collected more than eighty dollars!"

"That should buy a lot of new books," said Susan.

"Thanks for all your help," Tommy said. "I couldn't have done it without you."

"That's okay, Tommy," said Susan. "You're always helping me."

As Susan turned to leave, the schoolbooks and papers she was carrying fell to the floor. Tommy put the money envelope on the windowsill and bent down to help her pick them up.

"See? What did I just tell you?" Susan said with a grin.

Just then Nick ran up to them. "Tommy, weren't you supposed to meet your dad at work? You'd better get going right away."

Tommy hit his forehead with his palm. "I forgot I promised to help him after school today. See you tomorrow, guys," he called as he sped down the hall—leaving the money behind.

"Isn't this Roy Rogers coin neat?" Tommy said to Cousin Tilly, the receptionist at the Bailey Building and Loan. "I ordered it through the mail. It's going to be my good-luck charm."

"Yes, that's pretty swell, Tommy. Happy Trails to you, as Roy Rogers would say," said Cousin Tilly. "Now put it away and get those folders into alphabetical order before your father—oops, too late. Here he is now."

"Tommy, your teacher just called," said Mr. Bailey. "She asked about the library fund money. You were supposed to deliver it to the principal. What happened to it, son?"

Tommy hit his forehead again as he remembered that he'd left the envelope behind. "Oh, I know right where it is. Can I go back to school and bring it to the office?"

"Sure, but you'd better hurry. The school will be locked up soon. Do you want me to give you a lift?"

"No, Dad, you're busy. I'll run over and be back before you even know I'm gone."

But when he got there, he saw that the envelope was gone. *Where could it be?*

"Hello, Tommy. I just spoke with your father," said Tommy's teacher. "Did you get the money to the principal's office?"

"Uh . . ." Tommy didn't know what to say. "Not yet, Mrs. Welch. I'm just going there now."

"Oh, I'm afraid you're too late. It's all locked up. Why don't you give me the envelope for safekeeping tonight, and then we can meet in the office first thing tomorrow morning."

"I've got a better idea," said Tommy, walking backward down the hall. "I'll give it to my dad. He can keep it in the Building and Loan overnight. It *is* a bank, after all . . ." Tommy turned and sprinted off.

"But, Tommy . . ." said Mrs. Welch as he disappeared around the corner.

Tommy ran all the way to the bridge on the edge of town. He was desperate. He had no idea where the money had gone or how he could replace it by tomorrow morning.

"Please help me," he prayed with his eyes shut tight. "Everyone will think I stole it. My parents and friends will never forgive me."

When Tommy opened his eyes, a man was standing next to him. Tommy backed up a little. "Who are y-y-you?" he stuttered.

"Well, Tommy, I'm Arthur. Angel Second Class. I'm the answer to your prayer."

"How do you know my name?" Tommy asked suspiciously. "I'm not supposed to talk to strangers."

"I'm no stranger," said Arthur. "I'm your guardian angel, here to help."

"If you're an angel, where are your wings?" Tommy peered behind Arthur's back.

"I haven't won my wings yet," said Arthur. "But you'll help me, won't you?"

"I'm the one who needs help," said Tommy. "I need eighty dollars—and fast."

"We don't have money in Heaven," said Arthur.

"Then how am I going to fix this?" Tommy asked, tears welling up in his eyes. "I should just disappear."

"It's not worth running away for eighty dollars," said Arthur. "You don't realize how important you are to many people."

"Oh yeah?" said Tommy. "Well, tomorrow they're going to wish I had never been born. I *already* wish I had never been born!"

Arthur heaved a deep sigh. "Not this again. When will people ever learn? What do you think, Clarence?"

"Who's Clarence?" Tommy asked. "Who are you talking to?"

"Yes, Clarence, that'll do it," said Arthur. "Okay, you got your wish, Tommy. You were never born."

Just then a big swirl of wind came up, and the snow stopped falling.

Tommy reached into his pants pocket, then frantically checked his coat pockets.

"You aren't going to find your lucky coin," said Arthur. "You've never existed, so there's no coin."

"Great! I must have lost that, too," Tommy said angrily. "I *do* exist. I'm Tommy Bailey. I live at 320 Sycamore."

"There is no house at 320 Sycamore," said Arthur.

"I don't believe you!" said Tommy.

"Go see for yourself," Arthur suggested.

When they reached 320 Sycamore—or what *used* to be 320 Sycamore—there was no house there.

"What happened?" Tommy asked Arthur.

"The house burned down that Christmas Eve. You weren't around to tell your dad about the wall being hot. It was an electrical fire."

Tommy's mind reeled in confusion. "I don't get what's happening. Where's my family? Maybe Mrs. Carter will know something."

Arthur looked up toward the sky and said, "Now I see what you mean about this not being so easy, Clarence."

When Tommy rang the doorbell at Mrs. Carter's house, a stranger answered.

"Uh, hi, is Mrs. Carter home? I really need to talk to her," said Tommy.

"Mrs. Carter?" said the man. "She passed away last year, son. Sorry."

Arthur tried to explain as Tommy stumbled his way down the street. "Don't you see? You weren't there to get help that day when she fainted. . . . Each life touches so many others, if you aren't around, it leaves an awful hole."

Tommy ignored him. "I don't feel so good," he said. "Maybe Mr. Gower can help."

Tommy ran down the street and into Gower Drugs. A bell on the door rang as he opened it.

"Oh, somebody just made it," said Arthur from behind him. "Every time a bell rings, it means an angel got his wings."

Tommy was surprised that the old guy had kept up with him and wasn't out of breath at all. He approached the soda jerk and said, "Excuse me, is Mr. Gower in?"

"You must not be from around here. Mr. Gower doesn't own this place anymore."

"What do you mean? He always gives me free ice cream, ever since he got re-married. I introduced him to Mrs. Davis, and—"

The soda jerk interrupted. "Look, kid, I don't know what you're talking about. Mr. Gower never married anyone except Mrs. Gower. When she died, he gave everything up and moved to an old folks' home. He's a lonely old man."

"Tommy, you weren't there to introduce Mr. Gower to Mrs. Davis," Arthur explained patiently. "Don't you see how many people you helped? Even at your age, you've had a wonderful life."

Just then the Bailey family—George, Mary, Zuzu, Janie, and Pete—walked in.

Tommy ran to his parents. "Oh, Mom, Dad, I missed you so much. I thought you were—"

Mr. Bailey held Tommy at arm's length. The rest of the Baileys gave each other puzzled looks.

"I'm afraid you have us confused with someone else," Mr. Bailey said.

"Are you all right?" asked Mrs. Bailey. "Can we help you?"

Seeing the blank looks on his family's faces, Tommy panicked. "Don't you know me? It's Tommy, your son! What's happened?"

"Come on, Daddy," said Janie. "I want some ice cream."

Tommy turned to Arthur for help, but Arthur was nowhere to be seen.

Tommy raced back to the bridge where his prayers had been heard before.

"Please, Mr. Guardian Angel! I want everything to go back to how it was. I won't
ever think of running away again, I promise." He burst into tears. "Please help me get
back. I don't care if I get in trouble for losing the money. I'll pay it back somehow. I
just want to be Tommy Bailey again. Please, get me back."

Tommy looked up as snow began falling again. Hoping against hope, Tommy reached into his pocket . . . and found his lucky coin.

"Happy Trails!" he cried joyfully, punching the air.

Tommy ran home, passing all the spots he loved.
"Hello, Gower Drugs!"

As he passed Mrs. Carter's house, he saw her sweeping the walk.

"Hi, Mrs. Carter! I'll help you with that later. First I gotta get home."

"Hurry, Tommy," she answered. "They're all waiting for you."

Tommy burst open the front door of his house—yes, it was there!—to find his entire family, along with Susan, Nick, and Mrs. Welch. Tommy rushed into his parents' arms. This time they hugged him back.

"I love you, Mom and Dad!" Tommy exclaimed.

"My baby, my baby!" cried Mrs. Bailey.

Mr. Bailey said, "Tommy, your friends have something to say to you."

Susan looked a little sheepish. "Tommy, after you ran out of the school, I realized that you left the library money behind by mistake. I took it home with me, figuring we could turn it in to the principal tomorrow morning. When your mom called asking if I'd seen you, I brought it right over. I should have called earlier. I'm so sorry!"

"It's all my fault," Nick offered. "If I hadn't distracted you, you wouldn't have left it."

"No, no, don't blame yourselves. You're both good friends, and everything turned out okay in the end. Thank you so much," Tommy said.

Mr. Bailey said, "Someone once told me that no man is a failure who has friends.
Come on, everyone, it's dinnertime."

Just then Mrs. Bailey rang the dinner bell. "Food's on!"

"Every time a bell rings, an angel gets his wings," said Zuzu, taking her place at the table.

"That's right, Zuzu," Tommy said. He punched the air again and whispered, "Good going, Arthur!"